# LIGHTS OUT

## AMELIA MIRIAM REX

*"To everyone who hides their pain."*

# Contents

# Contents

# Book Playlist

*See You Again*
*(Wiz Khalifa, Charlie Puth)*
*Tonight Is The Night I Die*
*(Palaye Royale)*
*In The Stars*
*(Benson Boone)*
*jealousy, jealousy*
*(Olivia Rodrigo)*
*Maniac*
*(Conan Gray)*
*People You Know*
*(Selena Gomez)*
*Die first*
*(Nessa Barrett)*
*Favorite crime*
*(Olivia Rodrigo)*
*I miss you, I'm sorry*
*(Gracie Abrams)*
*Ghost Town*
*(Benson Boone)*
*Illicit affairs*
*(Taylor Swift)*
*No body, no crime*
*(Taylor Swift, HAIM)*
*Betty*
*(Taylor Swift)*

# 1

"Mom?"

Seventeen-year-old Ramona Grey called out to her mother from the top of the staircase.

She was hosting a sleepover for her four best friends, Ellen, Danielle, Quinn, and Bailey that night and was in desperate need of a quilt to finish setting up her room.

"Yes, Ramona?"

Her mom Lori answered from the kitchen where she was unpacking groceries.

"Where's my purple quilt? I can't find it", she asked.

"It's in the linen closet; I just took it out of the dryer and put it there."

Her mother answered while trying to fit a carton of milk into the already stuffed fridge.

Ramona ran downstairs and past the kitchen murmuring thanks to her mother as she passed her and opened the closet. She pulled the light purple quilt out of the closet and went back into the kitchen.

She dropped her quilt on a chair and went to see if there were any gems in today's groceries. As she scanned the snacks spread out on the kitchen island, her eyes stumbled upon a packet of microwave popcorn.

"Ooh!", she exclaimed picking up the packet to get a closer look at it.

"Salted butter! Nice choice Mom, the girls will love this!" Ramona put the packet back down, picked up the quilt, and ran back up.

*This was going to be the best sleepover ever!*

# 2

The doorbell rang just as Ramona turned on the ambiance lights in her room.

"Hi, Mrs. Grey"

Quinn's soft voice carried up the stairs.

"Hi, Girls!" Lori said.

"Ramona, they're here..." She called up.

"I know, I'm coming!" Ramona replied.

"Don't bother Ramona, we're coming up," Ellen said.

While she waited, Ramona pulled her pin-straight ginger hair into a messy bun and secured it with a claw clip. She had the best hair out of her friend group. Three of them were blondes except for Danielle who was Spanish and a brunette.

"We have arrived!"

Bailey announced as the girls stepped into her room and tossed their bags into a pile at the foot of Ramona's bed.

Suddenly, the sound of claws on wood floors excited all the girls.

"Luna!"

Ramona called out as her Golden retriever and best friend ran into her room. Everyone but Quinn was suddenly absorbed in playing with Luna.

"Luna, come here,"

Lori said with a leash in her hands.

"We have to go."
She said, hooking the leash onto the dog's collar.
Lori always took Luna to pet boarding when the girls came over.

Ramona was the first to notice that Quinn was sitting on a corner of her bed, worried-looking
eyes glued to her phone screen.
"Hey, Quinn!" Ramona asked,
"You, okay?" A concerned tone crept into her voice.
Quinn's head popped up at the sound of her name.
"Hmm, Yeah."
She said, sounding distracted.
"She's been like this since we got in the car,"
Danielle explained.
"Come on Quinn, Let's go to the pool," She said.
Ramona lived in California in a Beach house. So the pool was practically on the beach.
"Yeah, Let's go"
Quinn said, the ghost of worry still lingering on her face.

# 3

The view from the pool was like a painting. The sun shone brightly against a clear blue afternoon sky. While the girls were changing into their swimsuits, Lori made them some pink lemonade and kept it outside on a table under one of the beach umbrellas and the crystal glasses shimmered whenever they picked up a glass to take a sip.

Waves slowly lapped the shores of the beach, the soft smell of salt lingering in the air. So, basically, it was a perfect afternoon at the beach.

The girls put on sunscreen and jumped into the pool.
"Quinn, catch!"
Danielle said slowly swimming to the beach ball, but Quinn had already gotten out of the pool and was making her way to the chair where they left their phones, wrapping herself in a striped towel covering her pink and blue swimsuit. Her long, wet, blonde hair stuck to the towel.

"Quinn?" Ellen called out.
"Sorry, I got a text notification on my fit band and it's important; You guys have fun, I'll be right back"
Quinn replied picking up her phone from the chair and walking into the house.

But she didn't come right back, at least not until the rest of the girls had wiped themselves dry and ran to the beach to watch the sunset.

They did check on Quinn, of course, or they would be horrible friends. Every time, they found her sitting on the couch texting someone or on the phone, and every time they asked her to come back out, she just shooed them away, but now she was finally back, the sound of crunching sand under her feet as she came running to the beach, her footprints pressed into the sand behind her.

# 4

The sky got dark quickly after sunset and the girls ran indoors soon after. They changed into their sweat sets and turned on the TV, a bowl of popcorn on the coffee table in front of them.

Ramona opened her account on Netflix and flicked through her watchlist for a while until she reached the movie titled, '*Mean Girls*'.

The girls had been wanting to watch the movie for a long time but they never really got around to it.

"Ramona! You look just like Cady!"
Bailey exclaimed just a while after the movie began.

Ramona rolled her eyes. Apart from the red hair, there were no other similarities between the character and her, and Bailey knew that very well, but that's how their friendship worked because a few more minutes in, Ramona commented that Bailey looked like Regina, just to get back at her.

They finally got Quinn off her phone by forcing her to keep it on silent and they were all finally able to have some real fun, laughing, teasing, joking, and having the time of their lives.

The girls were halfway through the movie and the whole way through the bowl of popcorn when Ellen jumped up from the couch covering her mouth, ran to the bathroom, and slammed the door shut.

# 5

"Ellen, are you OK?"
Quinn asked, gently knocking on the bathroom door. The sound of retching came as a response.

"Mom," Ramona called.
"Ellen's sick." She finished.

Lori came running down the stairs and knocked on the door.
"Hey, Ellen, what's wrong?"
Lori asked, and, this time, as a response the door slowly creaked open and Ellen stood in front of them, all the color drained out of her face. Nobody said anything as Danielle walked Ellen over to the couch carefully.

"I'll go call your mom."
She said as soon as Ellen was seated and ran to grab her phone from the dining table where she left it.

"El, what happened?"
Bailey asked as the girls sat down next to her.
"I don't know... Must've been something I ate."
Ellen replied weakly, her voice almost a croak.

Ellen lied down on the couch while Ramona went to get some water for her. Ellen drank the water greedily and thanked Ramona, her voice sounding better now. Soon after, Danielle entered the room stuffing her
phone into the pocket of her grey sweatpants.

"Your mom said that you should just stay here. She thinks that driving home will make you feel worse. She said that she would come by to pick you up first thing in the morning."
She said joining the rest of them on the couch.
Ellen nodded weakly.

"You know what, let's just eat dinner and go to sleep," Quinn said.
"You'll be better in the morning El." She said to Ellen.

Ellen nodded, the loose strands of her blonde hair falling into her eyes.

All of them wanted nothing more than a good night's sleep.

# 6

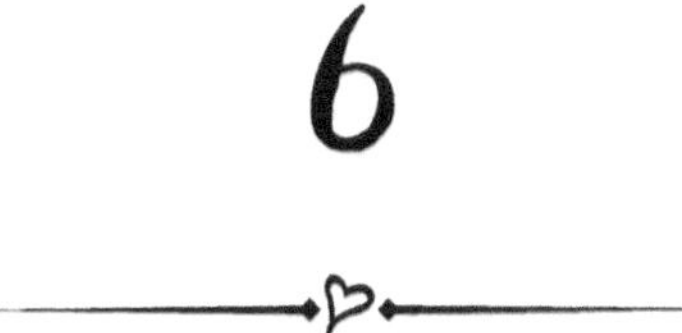

Sunlight entered the room through a small crack in the floral curtains. Ramona lay in bed for a while watching the dust swirl around in a small stream of light.

After a couple of minutes, she felt around her bedside table for her phone and grabbed it. She turned it on and checked the time.

It read *9:14 AM, Saturday.*

She felt a tinge of sadness. Her school was reopening in two days and then her life would go back to the same old schedule she had been following for the past three years. She pushed the thought out of her mind and sat up straight. She looked at her friends asleep peacefully in their sleeping bags, but someone was missing.

*Ellen.*

She figured she must be in the bathroom and got out of bed. She sleepily walked to the bathroom rubbing her eyes and knocked.

"Ellen?"

She called the word merging with a yawn.

*No response.*

"Ellen? Are you in there?" She asked again.

*Silence.*

Before knocking again, she saw that the lights were off. She tried the door. It was open. She carefully peeped inside.

The room was empty. Panic started creeping up on her as she ran to wake her friends.

"Danielle, wake up!"

She said shaking her friend a bit too aggressively.

Danielle slowly woke up

"What the ..."

she started but stopped when she saw the worry on Ramona's face.

"Ramona? What's wrong?" Danielle asked.

But Ramona had already moved on to waking Quinn and Bailey up.

"What happened?" Quinn asked.

Bailey sat up rubbing her eyes.

"It's Ellen. I can't find her." Ramona said.

"OK, Ramona, you need to calm down,"
Danielle said after Ramona explained how Ellen was not in the bathroom.

"Yeah, just because she is not in the bathroom doesn't mean she is missing."
Bailey piped up sleepily.

"Maybe she's in the kitchen, getting some water or something" Quinn suggested.

"Or maybe she went home. She is one to go home unannounced."
Bailey said spitefully, more to herself than to anyone else. Bailey and Ellen never really got along too well. It was a *friend-of-a-friend* kind of situation.

"Calm down, let's go and check the kitchen."
Danielle said, standing up.
Quinn stood up too.

Ramona cleared her head and slowly got up. Bailey was the last to stand, taking her own time stretching and yawning. After Bailey finally stood up, the girls rushed downstairs. They couldn't find Ellen in the kitchen or the living room.

Seeing the panic rising on Ramona's face, Quinn suggested that maybe Ellen went for a walk on the beach, sounding almost unsure of herself. The girls gave it a shot anyway, running out of the house, and calling Ellen's name.

By this time Lori had heard the noise and came down to check on them. The girls came back into the house after having no luck outside.

"What's wrong?" Lori asked.

"It's Ellen. She's gone!"

Ramona said on the verge of tears.

"Ramona, She probably went home. Her mom must've come early and she must have gone home. I'll call her mom and check if she's there." Lori said.

Ramona nodded.

After a few minutes, Lori stepped into the living room where the girls were sitting, pale as a ghost.

"Ramona."

She said with a voice too sweet to match the look on her face.

"Call the cops. Ellen is missing!"

# 8

"Yes officer, I understand. Thank you."
Ramona overheard her mother talking to the police in the kitchen. She picked up bits and pieces of the conversation by listening to her mother's side of it.
"But this is completely out of character for her."
Lori had said.
"Yes, I know it hasn't been long, but..."
She had said a few seconds later.
After saying thank you, Lori hung up.

"The police say that we jumped to conclusions too quickly in a panic. They said to try her phone, and wait a few more hours. They said if she doesn't show up by sundown, then we should give them a call."

Now that she thought about it, Ramona realized how stupid it was to not call her first, so they did. They waited a few seconds for the call to go through and suddenly, music started playing through the house echoing through the walls.

*It was Ellen's ringtone.*

The girls followed the music to Ramona's room. There, underneath Ellen's pillow on her makeshift sleeping bag made out of Ramona's quilt, they found Ellen's phone vibrating, the screen glowing with Bailey's contact.

It was a habit of Ellen's to forget her sleeping bag at almost every sleepover. It was also a habit of hers to keep her phone under her pillow. Helped her feel her alarm in the morning, she always said.

Bailey pressed the red decline button on Ellen's phone cautiously, almost as if she thought it would explode if she pressed it too quickly. Worry started showing up in Bailey's eyes too, at the sight of the phone. She dropped it on the pillow looking up at the girls, the black of her pupils taking over her blue eyes in fear.

Everyone was thinking the same thing, *where had Ellen gone without taking her phone?*

"Well, I guess I'll go keep this pillow back."
Quinn said to break the silence.
Danielle nodded slowly, eyes still on the phone.
Quinn picked the pillow up and went down to keep it back in the linen closet.

The rest of them sat there in silence staring at the phone, thinking about all the places Ellen could have vanished off to without taking her phone, until a blood-curdling scream broke through the silence.

# 9

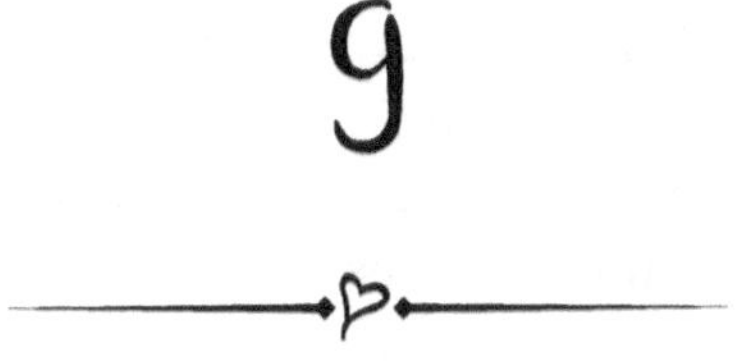

It was Quinn, screaming from downstairs.

Ramona and her mother almost bumped into each other, both heading downstairs as fast as their feet would let them.

"Quinn, where are you?"
Bailey called out, sounding truly concerned.

Quinn didn't have to answer, her heavy loud sobs could be heard through the whole house. They found her in front of the linen closet on her knees, Her sobs making her whole body shake.

"Quinn, what's wro..."
Lori started but let her sentence trail off, she didn't have to finish the sentence because when Quinn shuffled away, they could all see what was wrong.

Ellen lay there, in front of them all, motionless.

A bright red pool of blood around her head, her blonde hair now sticky and stained.

Ramona looked for the cause of the liquid, her eyes scanning the room for a carton of cranberry juice somewhere on the floor or counter. She couldn't process what was in front of her just yet, it had to be a prank, it just had to be, and clearly, her friends hoped so too.

All three of them just stood there, mouths open, for a long time until Quinn broke the silence.

"I found her in the closet, S-She's *bleeding*."
She said leaning on the word bleeding almost like it physically hurt her just to say the word.

Lori reacted first, moving towards Ellen and Quinn like a zombie, taking small tentative steps forward, almost as if she was approaching a wild bear.
She put her finger next to Ellen's nostrils and after a while, looked down.
Her body started shaking now too.

Ramona could feel tears stinging her eyes now and she let them fall to her cheeks because she finally understood what was happening right there in her kitchen.

*Ellen was dead.*

# 10

The police cared now because Ellen wasn't just gone for a day or two.

She was gone, forever.

The media seemed to care too. At least three news vans arrived in front of Ramona's house within an hour after Ellen's body was found. And around three more by the time the police finished their procedures and left the house.

Ramona sat on the couch with Danielle, Bailey, and Quinn like a statue, staring at her darkened reflection on her T.V.

She couldn't believe it. Who would ever hurt Ellen?

"All we can tell you right now is that the victim died of heavy bleeding from her head."

Police officer Alex Blair had said to the microphones when he got out of the house.

"We can't disclose any more information as of now but we will get back to you."

He said and waved the eager reporters away, as he made his way to his car.

"Girls, come have some breakfast, you can't just sit there all day."

Lori called to them, interrupting Ramona's thoughts.

Ramona heard the door click and turned to face her mother. Lori had been crying. She tried to cover it up but

Ramona saw right through it, but she didn't say anything. She didn't know what to say or do anymore. She would sit and cry for a while longer, but she really wasn't sure if she had any tears left to cry, so she got up, walking slowly to the dining table, the rest of the girls in tow. They all took seats in front of bowls of cereal with milk, but none of them ate. They couldn't eat.

Ramona just sat at the table for the next ten minutes, playing around with her spoon in the bowl of cereal until it became a soggy mess. She picked it up and walked over to the dumpster to throw the contents of the bowl away, but almost dropped it, startled, when the news reporters outside started shouting and making noise to get the attention of the person who had just arrived at the house. Ramona realized that they wouldn't need a house alarm for the next few weeks because the reporters would cause a ruckus every time someone stepped on the Grey's footpath.

"Mrs. Watson!"
Ramona heard over the clamor.
"How are you dealing with your daughter's demise?"
A reporter asked.

Ellen's mother had arrived.

# 11

Mrs. Watson was worse than Lori at hiding her tears. Even as she walked through the Grey's front door, she had been crying. Ramona didn't understand why. Ever since Ellen was young, she had spent way more time at Ramona's house than at her own. Even after her death, it had taken her mother hours to come and her father hadn't even left work yet.

"Oh Nancy, I'm so sorry."

Lori said, tears brimming her eyes now too.

She hugged Nancy tight and they sat like that for a while, both crying their eyes out. Once Lori finally let go, Nancy got up, eyeing the girls suspiciously.

"Tell me the truth. Which one of you killed my daughter?"

Nancy asked her voice breaking.

"We didn't do anything."

Danielle swore.

"Yeah, sure."

Nancy said under her breath.

The police had told the girls that they would be the main suspects because there were no signs of struggle or resistance. They assumed that Ellen knew the murderer and trusted them completely.

Ramona suspected her friends too. She didn't want to admit it to herself, but she did. She couldn't help it. Everything added up.

After another thirty minutes of crying, Nancy left the house. The sound of reporters mobbing her outside could be heard.

As she drove her Tesla away, the mob quietened down, leaving the house in silence once again, and as she got more and more time with herself, Ramona couldn't help suspecting her friends more and more too.

# 12

The day dragged on very slowly, and by evening, it started raining. The girls got ready for bed. Ramona's suspicion of her friends weighed down on her heart, she just couldn't shake the thought that she may be going to bed, completely letting her guard down with a murderer literally under her nose.

Bailey entered the room last and turned off the light. They climbed into bed and Ramona tried to go to sleep, counting sheep till she lost count and pressing her eyes closed so much that it hurt.

When she finally fell asleep, a dream about a faceless person pushing her friend in her dark kitchen popped into her mind. Slowly the faceless person started taking the form of Quinn, then Danielle, then Bailey.

She bolted upright. She couldn't help it anymore. She flicked the lights on and watched her friends get up.

"OK, for real, Which one of you did it? Which one of you killed Ellen?"

Ramona asked.

"Ramona, are you crazy? We didn't do anything!"

Quinn justified; tones of frustration and anger in her voice.

"No. I'm not. Admit it, even you guys have been suspicious of each other."

Ramona said.

"Well, if anyone is suspicious, it's you," Bailey said.

"And why is that?" Ramona asked.

"Inviting Ellen over to your house the night she died. Convenient, isn't it? You've probably been plotting this for months."

Bailey replied.

"I've invited you guys for multiple sleepovers. You can't just be suspicious of me because of a pure coincidence. Honestly Bailey, you hated Ellen, didn't you?"

Ramona retorted.

"That doesn't mean I would kill her."

Bailey shouted.

"What about Danielle, being extra nice to Ellen a few hours before she was killed, offering to call her mother when she got sick, she probably didn't even call her."

She said.

"Well, I'm sorry for being nice to a person who just threw up. And I called her mother, by the way. Mrs. Watson said she couldn't leave work."

Danielle said.

Ramona had never seen her this mad.

"And what about Quinn. She has been acting suspicious since Friday."

Danielle said.

"Yeah Quinn, what's your excuse?"

Bailey said accusingly.

"My parents are getting a divorce! How's that for an excuse?!"

Quinn shouted, tears falling down her cheeks. She buried her head into her pillow. The whole room was silent, The sound of rain hitting the roof tiles was the only sound to be heard for a long time.

"Quinn, I'm so sorry."

Bailey said.

"Yeah, well sorry isn't going to fix anything now, is it?"

Quinn said, wiping the tears from her eyes.

Ramona suddenly trusted her friends. She didn't know why. She just did.

The girls sat there on Quinn's sleeping bag, arms wrapped around each other for, minutes, hours, days, Ramona didn't know and she didn't care.

All that mattered was right now.

# 13

Sunday morning came too quickly. If Ramona was dreading going to school before, she hated the thought even more now.

The girls were staying over for a few more days. They really didn't feel like being away from each other. The last thing they wanted was to be in the face of suspicion without each other.

Ellen's funeral was going to be after school the next day. And so, another day went by. The girls were awake early on Monday morning because apparently, they weren't supposed to deal with grief by throwing away their own lives.

Guess how many times they had heard that before.

So, like every year, Ramona stepped into her pleated skirt and formal shirt. She looked at her reflection in her mirror. She looked okay at first glance, ginger hair falling over her shoulder covering the logo on her school uniform slightly, her pleated skirt resting just above her knees, but if you looked closer, actually looked, you would notice that her eyes looked empty, almost as if all emotion and hope had been drained out of them.

As they say, the eyes are the windows to the soul. Well, in Ramona's case, the windows had been shut, blackout blinds pulled over them.

Ramona and her friends walked out of the house, and as they expected, the reporters crowded around them as they got into Danielle's car.

Danielle put the key into the ignition and started the car, just like always, she drove to their school, just like always, and she pulled into the parking lot, just like always.

It was almost as if everything was normal, but it wasn't. *Nothing would be normal anymore.*

# 14

As the girls, minus Ellen, stood in the doorway, the clamor of voices stopped. All eyes were on them. Someone coughed and then the whispers began. They got nasty looks as they made their way to their lockers, but they stopped when they reached Ellen's old locker.

It was decorated almost as if it was a shrine for her.

*'You didn't deserve this'* one poster read.

*'We miss you, Ellen'*

was written on another poster with small red hearts drawn all over it.

Some others were not as sweet.

*'I will destroy the person who did this to you'*, was scrawled on another poster in black ink.

Ramona missed Ellen too but that was a bit too much she thought. The girls parted ways to go to their respective lockers.

Ramona made it past the whispers and finally reached her locker. She punched it in anger. She couldn't go on like this.

The metal vibrated under her knuckles and that's when the pain hit her. She grunted in pain and shoved her hand inside her skirt pocket.

She started unlocking her locker with her good hand and heard a voice from behind her.

"Whoa, that's got to hurt."

Ramona's cheerleading teammate Amanda walked up beside her.

"Have you heard what people are saying?"

She asked while fiddling with the lock on her own locker.

"They are saying that you or one of your friends murdered Ellen." She said.

"I know what they are saying."

Ramona said, grabbing books out of her locker and shoving them into her backpack.

"So?" Amanda asked.

"So what?"

Ramona asked making eye contact for the first time in the whole conversation.

"Did you do it?"

Amanda asked eagerly, her blue eyes sparkling, almost as if it was a perfectly normal thing to ask your teammate if they murdered their best friend.

"We didn't do anything."

Ramona said, slamming her locker door shut.

She walked away and Amanda caught up to her pretty soon.

"Okay fine," She said when she stepped beside Ramona, keeping pace with her.

"By the way, we need you to cheer today." She said.

"I really don't feel like cheering today."

Ramona said, picking up her pace.

"Please?"

Amanda said, going faster to stay next to Ramona.

"Donna is down with the flu. We're down a cheerleader." She said stopping.

Ramona sighed.

"I'll be there"
she called back, leaving Amanda alone in the middle of
the hallway.

# 15

Ramona really didn't think she would go for cheer, but there she was on the top of a pyramid in her cheer uniform, hair pulled into a tight ponytail.

"OK girls, let's not forget to smile", their coach said.

Ramona felt the words like a punch to her gut. After that everything that happened was a blur.

Ramona did a backflip off of the pyramid and her hair whipped at her face.

The next thing she knew, she was on the ground, a shooting pain going through her entire body starting at her ankle. She gripped at it, her eyes flooding over with tears of pain.

"Ramona, are you okay?"

Her coach ran to her, while the rest of the team disassembled their human pyramid and came to check on her.

"No..." Ramona choked out. "I-I think I sprained it."

She said, tears falling on her white uniform top.

She was rushed to the nurse's office where she was given an ice pack.

She sat there for a while icing her ankle and then fell asleep. She had the same dream again, a faceless man killing her friend, except this time they stayed faceless.

Suddenly, that faceless man turned to face Ramona and before she could run away, they tapped her on the shoulder and called her name. She woke up to see Danielle looming over her.

"Ramona?"

She said, tapping Ramona's shoulder.

"Are you alright?"

She asked when Ramona opened her eyes.

"Yeah, I'm fine, just a little sprain," Ramona said.

"What time is it?" She asked.

"Time to go home," Danielle said.

"Quinn and Bailey are waiting in the car." She said.

"Oh, alright."

Ramona said. She tried to get out of bed but winced when her foot hit the ground.

"Let me help you."

Danielle said, offering Ramona a hand to use as a crutch.

Ramona took Danielle up on her offer and walked, putting the pressure off her hurt leg on Danielle's elbow, past the Ellen shrine, and out the doors.

Ellen would have been the one to help her. She was the strongest. But she would never be able to help Ramona with her cheer injuries anymore.

*She wouldn't be able to do anything anymore.*

# 16

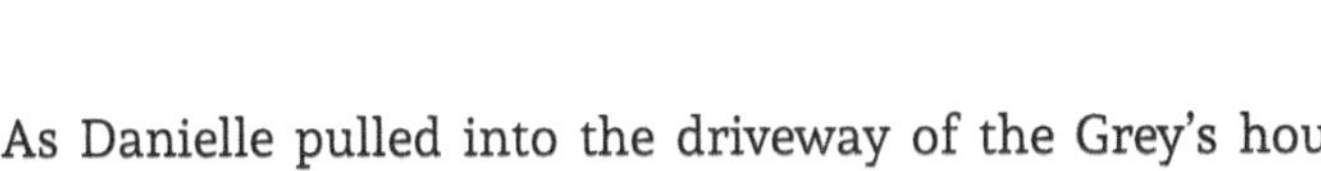

As Danielle pulled into the driveway of the Grey's house, Ramona realized how weird her life would be from now on. The sleepover on Friday already felt like an eternity away.

A memory too distant to be close. It was truly a night to remember but for all the wrong reasons.

Everything was against them that night, but there was no point thinking about it now. That night was over. She could never go back to it. She could never live it again.

The last normal night of her life. The word normal was popping into her mind a lot, wasn't it? Even though nothing was.

"Ramona?"

Lori's voice cut into her thoughts.

"Ramona, let me help you."

Bailey said and Quinn took Ramona's backpack from her side, shouldering it, her own bag in her hand.

Bailey carefully got Ramona out of the car and walked her over to the house. Danielle held the front door open as Bailey led Ramona to the couch followed by Quinn with her backpack which she dropped near the couch where Bailey was helping Ramona hoist her leg onto the couch.

"I'll get you some ice."

Danielle said the door closing behind her.

Lori entered the living the same time that Danielle left.

"What happened?"

She said when she saw Ramona with her foot elevated on a pile of sofa cushions.

She opened her mouth to answer, but Quinn was quicker.

"She sprained her ankle at cheer practice."

She said, staring at Ramona's hurt ankle, almost like she was trying to see through Ramona's pale skin.

"Oh Ramona, you should be more careful."

Her mother said.

She couldn't focus. How could she? She couldn't smile. She couldn't pretend to be happy. Not when her best friend was gone.

Ramona couldn't say dead. She wasn't dead. She was gone. She would see her, someday when Ramona was gone too.

Danielle came back with a bag of frozen peas.

"I couldn't find anything else."

She said looking apologetic. It wasn't her fault that the Grey's fridge was filled with a whole bunch of garbage, Ramona thought as she slowly placed the ice on her ankle.

"Ramona, does this mean you can't come for the funeral?"

Lori asked from behind the couch.

"No. I'll come." Ramona said.

She wouldn't miss her last chance to see her friend's face.

Her last chance to say goodbye, no, 'see you later', whether Ellen could hear her or not.

# 17

Three hours later, Ramona was still sitting on the couch, except this time she was in the black dress that she somehow managed to wear.

The shoes were a whole other problem and she just couldn't figure out how to wear any of her fancy-looking shoes without them hurting her ankle, so she chose comfort over looks and pulled on her flip-flops.

The girls all got into Lori's car and drove to the cemetery.

Ramona hadn't been to a cemetery since her father's funeral. No. She shouldn't think about her father, it had hurt her too much back when she was a small child and it still hurt her now and that was the last thing she needed, more pain.

They got out of the car and walked over to the burial spot.

Well, the others walked, Ramona limped, holding on to her mother's hand for balance.

There, in a coffin, covered with hundreds and hundreds of flowers was Ellen. She looked like she was peacefully asleep.

How many times had Ramona taken photos of Ellen when she was actually just asleep?

She should go home and check.

"Oh," Nancy said, walking up to them.

"You came."

She said, sounding slightly disappointed.

A man walked up behind Nancy. It took Ramona a while to recognize him, but she did, eventually.

It was Ellen's father, who was absent for most of her childhood, he had finally made it.

A memory popped into Ramona's head as she eyed him with spite. Ellen had come running to Ramona's house on her sixth birthday, her face streaked with tears. Her father couldn't make it, and her mother would be coming home late.

Ramona and her mother were the ones who were there to console her. That evening, Lori took them both to an ice cream shop and bought them huge bowls of ice cream.

Ellen got used to it eventually, her parents missing birthdays, school meets, holidays, everything, and over the years, Ellen started spending more and more time at Ramona's house.

She was more than just Ramona's best friend; She was like her sister.

That thought stirred something in Ramona. She let more of her tears fall to the ground.

# 18

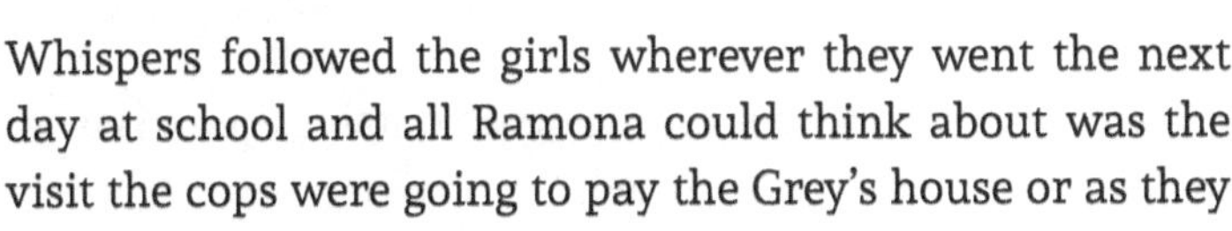

Whispers followed the girls wherever they went the next day at school and all Ramona could think about was the visit the cops were going to pay the Grey's house or as they called it, the crime scene.

Would they ever be able to figure out what happened to Ellen? Would they ever find out who made Ellen go?

"Ramona, did you hear me?"

A voice said. Ramona had completely forgotten she was in English class. The voice was her teacher.

How long had she been calling her? Ramona had been so lost in her own thoughts that she forgot she had to make it through five more hours of school before she could go home again

"Yes sorry, can you repeat the question."

Ramona said, her mind slowly coming back to reality.

"I didn't ask you a question." Her teacher said.

She could practically hear the eye roll in her voice.

"You had been staring at the same corner for so long, I started to get worried."

She finished.

Usually, her classmates would have laughed at her, but this time they just stared at her.

Ramona couldn't tell what their expressions were exactly, but she knew that it wasn't anything good.

As soon as Ramona was about to answer with some bad excuse, The bell rang, and everyone jumped up from their seats.

"Today's homework,"

Her teacher started, shouting to be heard over the shuffling footsteps and scraping chairs.

"Is to read chapter 20, in your books." She said.

Ramona wasn't going to read that. She couldn't with cops running around her house.

"Hey,"

Amanda caught up with her again outside their class.

"How's your leg?" She asked.

"I'm walking again."

Ramona said dryly. Her leg had gotten better after a good night's sleep.

"Oh, good!"

Amanda said, her enthusiasm way too inappropriate for this conversation.

"So can you come for cheer today?" She asked.

"Can't; the cops are coming to my house today. I have to be there." Ramona replied.

"Oh, OK," Amanda said.

"Well, I'll see you tomorrow!" Amanda said.

"Yeah, sure."

Ramona said, walking to her math class.

Did she really want to be at her house when the cops were there rummaging through all of Ellen's stuff? Easy answer, *no*.

Did she prefer going home over cheering when all she felt like doing right now was burying her face in a pillow and screaming? Another easy answer, *yes*.

# 19

Officer Alex arrived soon after the girls got home, and he wasn't alone. A pretty, pale woman with her black hair pulled into a neat bun stood behind him. She was in a police uniform, the blue fabric forming small wrinkles where she had tucked her shirt into her pants with a belt holding them up.

"Good evening, Mrs. Grey."

Officer Alex said when Lori opened the door.

"This is Officer Abigail Stone."

He said, Stepping aside to reveal her.

She took a small step forward and held out a hand for Mrs. Grey to shake it. She took it, giving it two gentle shakes.

"Nice to meet you officer."

Lori said, taking her hand back.

"Please come in." She said.

"Can I get you anything? Coffee? Water?"

She asked as they entered the house.

"No, thank you." Officer Abigail said.

Her soft voice carried itself through the whole house.

"This is a nice house, Mrs. Grey."

Officer Alex said. Lori nodded in agreement.

"Thank you." She said quietly.

"Do you have security cameras?" He asked.

"Yes, we have one up front. That's all though." She said.

"Can we have a look at Friday night's footage?" He asked.
Ramona thought it was more of an order than a request.
"Yes of course." She said.
"Ramona!" She called.
Ramona who had been watching from the couch flinched.
"Can you please get me my laptop?" Lori said.
Ramona bolted up the stairs. She needed answers, and she would do anything to get them. If this was the first step towards them, then she was happy to help.

# 20

Luna followed Ramona down.

"Oh! Who's this?"

Officer Abigail exclaimed, bending over to stroke the friendly dog's golden fur.

"This is our dog, Luna," Lori explained.

"And she didn't notice anyone in the house the night Ellen died?" Officer Alex asked, looking slightly afraid of the huge ball of furry gold in front of him.

"No, she wasn't here. I had her at pet boarding that night because I didn't want her going in and disturbing the girls."

Lori said as Ramona handed her the laptop.

Officer Alex nodded.

"All right." Lori said placing the laptop on the kitchen island.

She pressed the power button and the machine came to life, a bright picture of a man sitting with a dog put as the wallpaper.

"Who is that?"

Officer Abigail asked pointing to the tall man in the photo.

Ramona knew who he was. It was her father, a man she hadn't quite gotten to know well enough.

"That was my husband. He passed away when Ramona was seven."

Lori explained, her voice cracking.

"I'm so sorry."

Officer Abigail said, looking like she regretted asking the question.

On the other hand, Officer Alex showed no difference in emotion.

Lori clicked away from the home screen and swiftly typed in her password when the box popped up. She moved the cursor around until it found the security camera application and clicked on it.

She then turned the screen completely to the cops and left them to it.

"I had checked the footage. I didn't see anything out of the ordinary."

She said a few moments after Officer Alex started clicking around on the laptop, Officer Abigail leaning over his shoulder to get a better look.

Around thirty minutes later, Officer Alex looked up from the screen.

"You were right Mrs. Grey. There is nothing on here." He said

"Do you always keep the back door closed?" Officer Abigail asked.

"Always," Lori said.

"And there are no broken windows?" Officer Alex asked.

"None," Lori confirmed.

"Does anyone else have the keys?"

Officer Abigail asked, catching on to where Officer Alex was going with this.

"No of course not. We don't even keep a spare outside."

Lori said, starting to look nervous.

"Before we go, can we please see Ellen's phone and bag? A teenager's belongings can give us many clues about

them."
Officer Abigail said.

# 21

"Everything looks normal here so far…"

Officer Abigail said, rummaging through Ellen's new purple duffel bag. She got new things like meals, she probably had more clothes than an entire mall store, and a closet to match.

It was too bad that the last one she saw was the Grey's stuffy linen closet.

"What's this?"

Officer Abigail said pulling out a piece of crumpled-up paper from Ellen's makeup bag.

Officer Abigail opened the paper and started to read off of it; "I'm going to get back at you Ellen" she read.

"Do you recognize this handwriting?"

She asked handing the note to Danielle. She examined the note.

"Yeah, It's Blake's, isn't it?"

She said pointing the note in Ramona's direction.

"Yeah," Ramona said.

"Blake was Ellen's ex-boyfriend, and we have all borrowed his notes. Whatever you say about the guy, he does take really good notes."

Bailey explained.

"I think we should have a little chat with him."

Officer Abigail said looking at Officer Alex

"Can we see her phone?" Officer Alex asked.

"Of course." Lori said.

Ramona was already opening the drawer of her bedside table and fishing Ellen's phone out of it.

"Here,"

She said, handing it over to Officer Alex.

He powered it on and sighed.

"It's password locked." He said.

"I guess we can just take it to the station."

Officer Abigail said, standing up after zipping Ellen's bag closed and swinging it over her shoulder

"Along with this",

she said tilting her head towards the bag.

She pulled out a small plastic zip-lock bag out of her pocket and gave it to Officer Alex, who opened it and dropped the phone inside.

"We are leaving now." Officer Alex said.

"We'll get back to you the second we find something," He said.

And they were gone. Leaving Ramona to her thoughts again. It was worse now because all the girls had gone back home. Sure she could call them, but how much help would that be?

She was alone. She had to get out of the house. Out of her head. She could go for a light jog she thought. Yeah, That was a good idea.

She pulled her headphones off her desk and put them around her neck. She stuffed her phone into her hoodie pocket and made her way downstairs.

# 22

The smell of her own sweat lingered in the air around her as Ramona jogged the length of the beach all the way to her house.

The last of the news vans had left her front yard that afternoon, but she still went in through the back just so she could see the waves as she ran, just a bit farther away than the point at which to ocean met the shores.

She reached the back door of her house, slotted her keys in, and opened it. She abandoned her dirty shoes next to the door and opened her phone to turn off her music and saw a lot of texts.

About ten of them were from people who treated her like wallpaper till Friday, including Amanda.

Ramona swiped notifications away until she saw one from Danielle.

'Hi Ramona! Bailey, Quinn, and I are going for milkshakes, wanna join?' It read.

'Sure, I'll meet you there' Ramona typed in and pressed send.

A chocolate milkshake would be great to get her mind off of everything.

Ramona quickly took a shower and pulled on her comfiest pair of jeans and a beige sweatshirt, her wet hair, looking darker than usual, sticking to it up to the middle of her back.

She stared at herself in the mirror as her blow dryer blew her hair around. Her bright green eyes had small dark circles underneath them.

She never wore makeup but this time, she grabbed a bottle of her mom's concealer dabbed a few drops under her eyes, and blended it in sloppily.

She shrugged as she looked back in the mirror.

It was better than looking like she had black paint under her eyes, she thought as she looked closely at her cakey makeup.

She pulled her now dry hair into a messy bun, grabbed her keys off her bedside table, and closed her bedroom door behind her.

# 23

Ramona knew exactly where to go; 'Coastal Creamery'.

It was a small ice cream store near the beach, though, it was more famous for its milkshakes.

Ramona's pale beige sweatshirt kept her body safe from the cold but the wind blew against her face, hitting it like a million little arrows.

It was only after Ramona was halfway to the shop that she realized how eerily similar the sweatshirt she was wearing was to the one that Ellen had been wearing when she had been murdered.

Ramona crossed her arms over her chest and walked on. The shop was small but roomy, painted white with a blue stripe running all around it.

Ramona pushed the door open, a small bell jingling as the top of the door hit it.

Ramona found the girls and sat down next to them. Almost immediately, the waitress, Jasmine made her way to their table, her long straight black hair pulled into a high ponytail.

"Ramona!" She exclaimed. Jasmine was a senior at their school. The eighteen-year-old had helped Ramona out of several tough situations.

"How are you?" She said.

"Not good," Ramona said.

Jasmine didn't reply. Instead, she pulled Ramona into a small side hug, the soft Lilac fabric of Jasmine's shirt pressing against her face.

Ramona inhaled the smell of generic fabric softener. She felt safe next to Jasmine.

"Shall I get you your usual?"

Jasmine asked, smiling.

"Yes, that's perfect, thank you." Danielle said.

# 24

Ramona had no idea how she made it through another tormenting day at school. Actually, she had no idea how she made it through another day.

Every time she walked through her house, she was reminded of the two closest people she had lost; Her father and Ellen.

Pictures of her father hung all around her house but she really only had memories about one of them. It was taken at the beach, soon after they had moved in.

All of them, even her brother, Rodger, another person she didn't get the chance to know well.

Everything was perfect, the sun was shining, and the waves as blue as the sky. Ramona tore her eyes away from the picture.

At least she got to see Ellen's body, she thought.

Her father died in a fire, He was at a party with five other people, all of them died, their bodies were never found. Ramona's father's ashes were the only thing left to bury.

She climbed up to her room and scrambled into her bathroom. She washed her face and reached for her towel, only to realize it wasn't there.

Ramona walked out of the bathroom, water dripping onto her shirt from her face.

"Mom?"

she called from her doorway.

"Where's my towel?" she asked.

"I kept it for washing."

Her mother called back up.

"I think there is an unused one in the guest bathroom."

She said after a while.

"Come get that one." She finished.

Ramona rolled her eyes and dragged herself down the stairs. She reached for the door handle and twisted it open. She flicked on the lights, walked in, and grabbed the towel from the towel rod.

She flipped the toilet seat down with her leg and walked out but stopped dead in her tracks when she realized what she had just done.

A thousand thoughts came rushing into her mind all at once.

# 25

Ramona found herself knocking on a dark wooden door. It opened with a creak and a tall man with familiar green eyes greeted her.

"Hello Rodger."

Ramona said flatly.

"Ramona, what are you doing here?" Rodger asked.

"What? A girl can't meet her brother who killed her best friend anymore?"

She asked, her tone oozing with sarcasm.

"Ramona, come inside...please." He said.

Ramona could hear the panic rising in his voice. She stepped inside and crossed her arms.

"Ramona, let me explain."

Rodger said, looking straight at Ramona.

"What's there to explain Rodger, you killed Ellen!"

Ramona said, almost shouting.

Although Rodger towered over her, she still felt more powerful than him.

"Ramona, please."

Rodger said, tears threatening to spill over from his eyes at any moment.

# 26

**Ellen**

The darkness of Ramona's room greeted me when I opened my eyes. It was still early, but I was thirsty. I got up and stepped into my slippers and carefully made my way down the stairs to the kitchen. I wrapped my hands around my body and shivered a bit as I entered the cold kitchen. "Ellen!" a voice called quietly from the cloak of darkness. I gasped as I realized who it was... Rodger. "I already told you, Rodger, we're over," I said, facing away from the voice. "Ellen, I'm sorry." He said. I knew he was using me; he just wanted my money. I turned towards the voice and caught his bright green eyes glinting in the dark. "Why did you block my number?" He asked, impatience creeping into his voice. That's when I heard it, the slight slurring in his voice that I had become too used to. He was drunk. I kept quiet. "Ellen?" he said, his voice becoming more urgent now. My eyes moved down to his feet. "Are you seeing someone else?" he asked me. "Yes," I said, I never even knew I could make my voice so quiet. I dared to look back up at his eyes, but I regretted it immediately, there was a shift in them, like a fire had been set ablaze behind them. He charged at me and before I could even understand what was happening, I felt two firm hands push against my shoulders. I stumbled and fell backward, and something hit me. I don't know what exactly, but it hurt, it hurt like a million little swords jabbing into my head all at the same time, I felt the back of my *head just before I slumped down onto the ground. I brought my hand in front of my face; It was covered in bright red blood. I fell to the floor and lay there looking up at the ceiling. Rodger was looking at me. He looked scared. Everything was blurry, and the tears stinging my eyes were insufficient for the pain I was feeling. Rodger picked me up and carried me somewhere. He pushed me into a closet, I think, and shut the door. As I stared at the closed door, I felt all life slip out of me. I pressed my eyes shut and let the tears spill out of them. I took a deep breath. Breathing hurt, like squeezing my lungs beyond a limit they were never supposed to reach. Everything hurt, and suddenly, it all stopped. Everything stopped.*

# 27

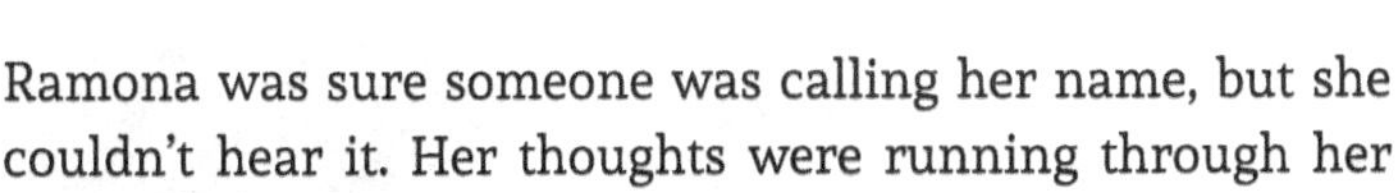

Ramona was sure someone was calling her name, but she couldn't hear it. Her thoughts were running through her mind like a freight train.

"Why?"

Ramona heard herself say, but she couldn't be sure that any noise escaped her mouth.

"I loved her," Rodger said.

"And I was drunk." He added quickly.

Ramona felt for a chair, and when she couldn't find one, she let her limp body slump to the floor.

He waited a minute before asking

"How did you know?"

"You left the toilet seat up", Ramona said.

"Oh." He said looking down at his muddy shoes.

"Ramona,"

Rodger said, joining her on the soft, carpeted floor.

"I'm so, so sorry."

He said, tears streaking his cheeks.

"I-it was an accident."

He said, his voice cracking now.

"I know", Ramona said getting up.

She could see the hope in her brother's face. She grabbed the door handle,

"But you let it happen", Ramona said pulling open the door and stepping out.

"She was the one who was there for me when you weren't. And you let her die."

Ramona glared at him

"You mean nothing to me."

She slammed the door shut and ran faster than she ever had. Away from their house, away from the place where Ellen's killer lived.

*Just away.*

# 28

## Epilogue

It was five months after everything happened. The sun was shining, the waves were a bright blue and glittering like a million little sapphires. It was a perfect day at the beach.

Ramona sat on a beach towel, a glass of pink lemonade in her hand. She could feel the sand against her skin from below the thin fabric of the towel as she watched her friends playing in the waves, splashing each other with salty water.

"Ramona, come on!" Danielle called.

"The water's warm," Bailey said, laughing.

Ramona smiled, got up, and ran towards them.

Quinn's parents had divorced two months ago but she was taking it fine.

Ramona did miss Ellen a lot, but she had moved on.

She didn't miss her brother at all, she really meant what she had told him the last time she saw him.

He meant nothing to her, but her friends, this day, this bright sunny day meant everything to her.

# Acknowledgments

I don't even know what to say! This last year has had its ups and downs and many of the ups are all thanks to my supportive family and even more supportive readers. First of all, I would like to thank my Grandfather, Antony Maliakal, who sadly never got to read this book. I owe everything to him. The first poem I ever wrote was for him. His encouragement was what kept me going, and I can only hope that his spirit will keep me going from heaven. I would like to thank the rest of my grandparents, Stephini Antony, Omana Joseph, and Joseph Kaippillil, for their unending support. A special thanks has to be given to my parents, Roopa Maliakal and Rex George, for the way they both helped me through all the problems I faced while writing this book. My cousins, Aanya Anil, Ayana Anil, and Ishaan B Joseph, also deserve a special mention, not only for inspiring me to start writing with a book based off on them ("The Mysterious Explosion") but also for always being there for me. I would especially like to thank Ishaan for being my biggest, little fan and asking me when my next book would come out every time I saw him. I would also like to thank my cousins from my father's side Naina Leslie and Ian Leslie for their support. I just have to thank my best friend Diya D M. I had just met her the year I wrote my first book and she, along with a few of my other classmates was extremely supportive of my writing journey.

Last but not least, I would like to thank all of you for supporting me and my small books. I hope that you all enjoyed this one.

With love,

Amelia <3